## Written by
## Jon Scieszka

Characters and environments developed by the

David Shannon   Loren Long   David Gordon

## Illustration Crew:

Executive producer

TOT
INDUSTRIES

in association with

ANIMAGIC S.L.

Creative Supervisor

**Sergio Pablos**

Drawings by

**Juan Pablo Navas**

Color by

**Isabel Nadal**

**Gabriela Lazbal**

Art direction by

**Dan Potash**

**Laurent Linn**

Jon Scieszka's
TRUCKTOWN

Truckery Rhymes

# Simon & Schuster Books for Young Readers

NEW YORK    LONDON    TORONTO    SYDNEY

SIMON & SCHUSTER BOOKS FOR YOUNG READERS
An imprint of Simon & Schuster Children's Publishing Division
1230 Avenue of the Americas, New York, New York 10020

Book design by Laurent Linn and Dan Potash
The text for this book is set in Futura BT.
The illustrations for this book are rendered digitally.
Manufactured in China
2 4 6 8 10 9 7 5 3

Library of Congress Cataloging-in-Publication Data
Scieszka, Jon.
Truckery rhymes / by Jon Scieszka ; artwork created by
the Design Garage—David Gordon, Loren Long, David Shannon.—1st ed.
p. cm.—(Jon Scieszka's Trucktown)
ISBN: 978-1-4169-4135-4
1. Children's poetry, American. 2. Nursery rhymes, American.
3. Trucks—Juvenile poetry. I. Gordon, David, ill.
II. Shannon, David, ill. III. Long, Loren, ill. IV. Design Garage.
V. Title.
PS3569.C5748B54 2009
811'.54—dc22
2007037439

first edition

1109 SCP

To Dan P., who knows how to dress a truck

—J. S.

# CONTENTS

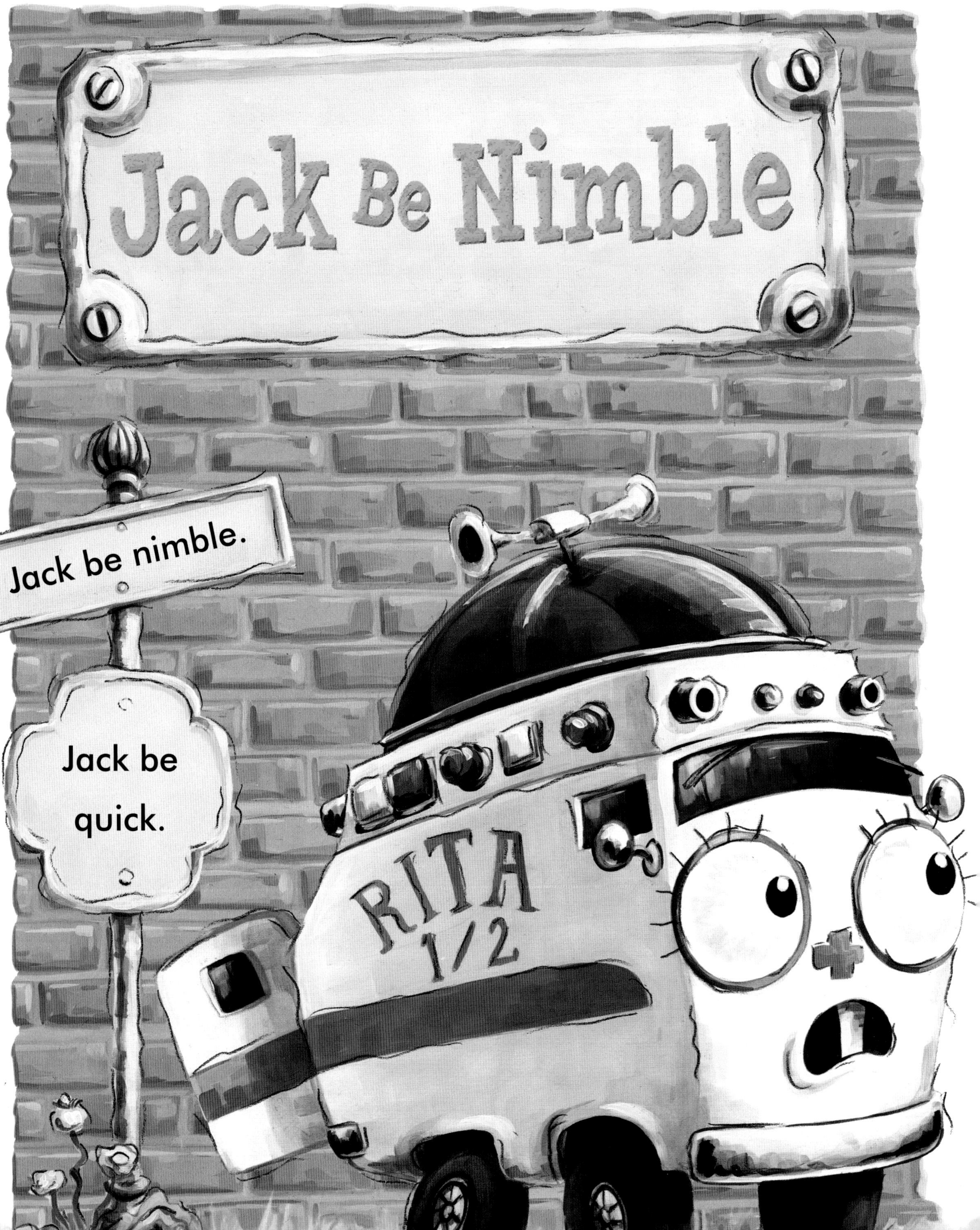
Jack Be Nimble
Jack be nimble.
Jack be quick.
RITA 1/2

Jack smash through
the wall of brick.

# Little Dan Dumper

Little Dan Dumper sat on his bumper,
Taking his break for the day.

Along came Pete Loader,

who revved his loud motor,

And frightened Dan Dumper away.

# Rumble, Rumble, Monster Max

Rumble, rumble, Monster Max.

Can you jump those junkyard stacks?

Up above the trash so high,

Like a rocket in the sky.

Rumble, rumble, Monster Max.

Yep, he jumped those junkyard stacks.

# Three LOUD Trucks

Three LOUD trucks.
Three LOUD trucks.
See how they ZOOM.
See how they ZOOM.
They all jumped over
the *muck and goo*.
They skidded and screeched
and their mufflers blew.
Did you ever see
such a crazy crew?
As three LOUD trucks.
Three LOUD trucks.

# Rock-a-Bye Mixer

Rock-a-bye mixer at the site top.

When the wind blows, the building will rock.

14

When the beam breaks, the mixer will fall.

And down will come Melvin—
bricks, beams, and all.

# This Is the Way

This is the way we **scoop** the dirt,
scoop the dirt, **scoop** the dirt.
This is the way we **scoop**
the dirt, every
Trucktown morning.

This is the way we **dump** the dirt,
dump the dirt, **dump** the dirt.
This is the way we **dump** the dirt,
every Trucktown morning.

This is the way we **smooth** the dirt,
smooth the dirt, **smooth** the dirt.
This is the way we **smooth** the dirt,
every Trucktown morning.

This is the way we **zoom** and **play** . . .
every Trucktown morning.

# EENIE MEANIE

Eenie meanie mynie mo.

If you see Big Rig, you should go.

# MYNIE MO

He will chase you—don't be slow.
Eenie meanie mynie . . . MO!

# GABBY Had a LITTLE BEAR

Gabby had
a little bear—

Its fur was
soft and brown.

And everywhere
that Gabby went,

She took
her bear to town.

Peter Peter Payload Eater

Hit a rock and blew his heater.

He roared into the lake and fell.

And there he cooled off very well.

The wheels on the truck
go **round** and **round**,

**Round** and **round**,
**Round** and **round**.

The wheels on the truck
go **round** and **round**,

all through the town.

The scoop on the truck
　　goes CHOMP, CHOMP, CHOMP,
CHOMP, CHOMP, CHOMP,
CHOMP, CHOMP, CHOMP.
The scoop on the truck
　　goes CHOMP, CHOMP,
　　CHOMP,
　　all through the town.

The blade on the truck
　　goes *scrape, scrape, scrape,*
*Scrape, scrape, scrape,*
*Scrape, scrape, scrape.*
The blade on the truck
　　goes *scrape, scrape, scrape,*
　　all through the town.

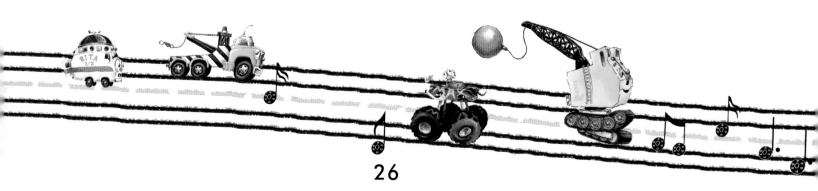

The bell on the truck

    **goes** ding, ding, ding,

Ding, ding, ding,

Ding, ding, ding.

The bell on the truck

    **goes** ding, ding, ding,

    all through the town.

The siren on the truck

    goes ***whoop***, ***whoop***, ***whoop***,

***Whoop***, ***whoop***, ***whoop***,

***Whoop***, ***whoop***, ***whoop***.

The siren on the truck

    goes ***whoop***, ***whoop***, ***whoop***,

    all through the town.

The ice-cream truck goes . . .

Do you want an ice cream?

Do you want an ice cream?

Do you want an ice cream?

Do you want an ice

cream?

All the trucks go:

"Izzy, you are messing up the song."

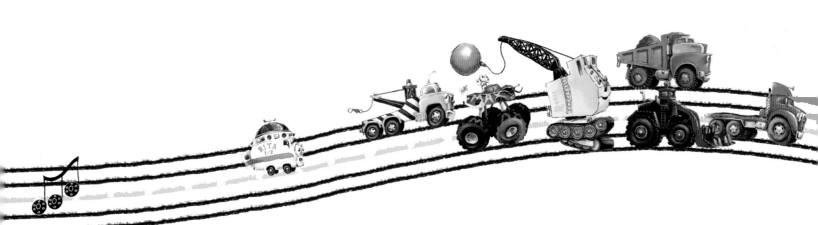

The ball on the truck
goes **BAM, BAM, BAM**.

The engine on the truck

goes VROOM, VROOM,

VROOM.

The cruncher on the truck
goes crunch, crunch,
crunch.

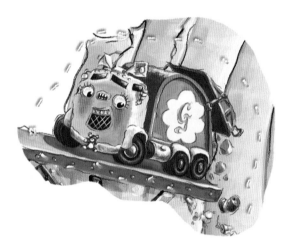

The pipes on the truck
go BRAAAP, BRAAAP,
BRAAAP,
all through the town.

The flap on the truck
goes **BOOM, BOOM, BOOM**.

The drum on the truck
**goes** whoosh, whoosh, whoosh.

The hook on the truck
goes **clank, clank, clank**.

The horn on the truck
**goes** *b w e e p ?  b w e e p ?
b w e e p ?*
all through the town.

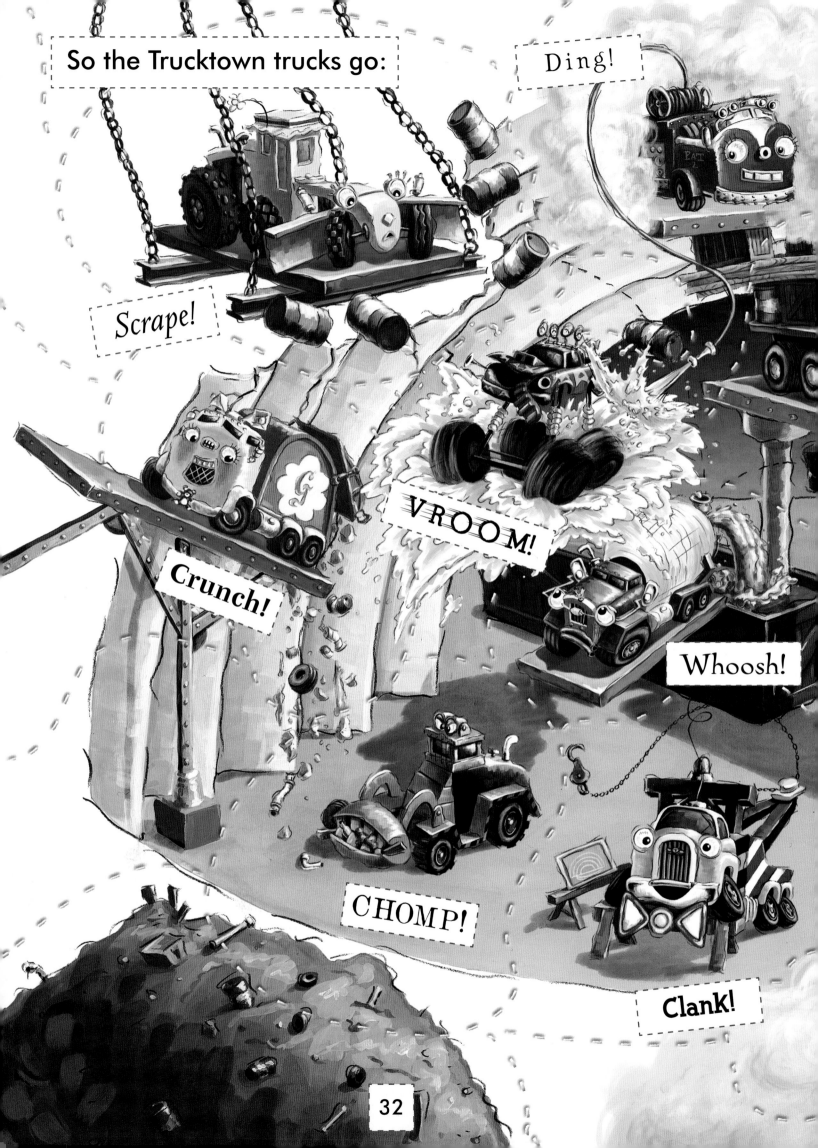

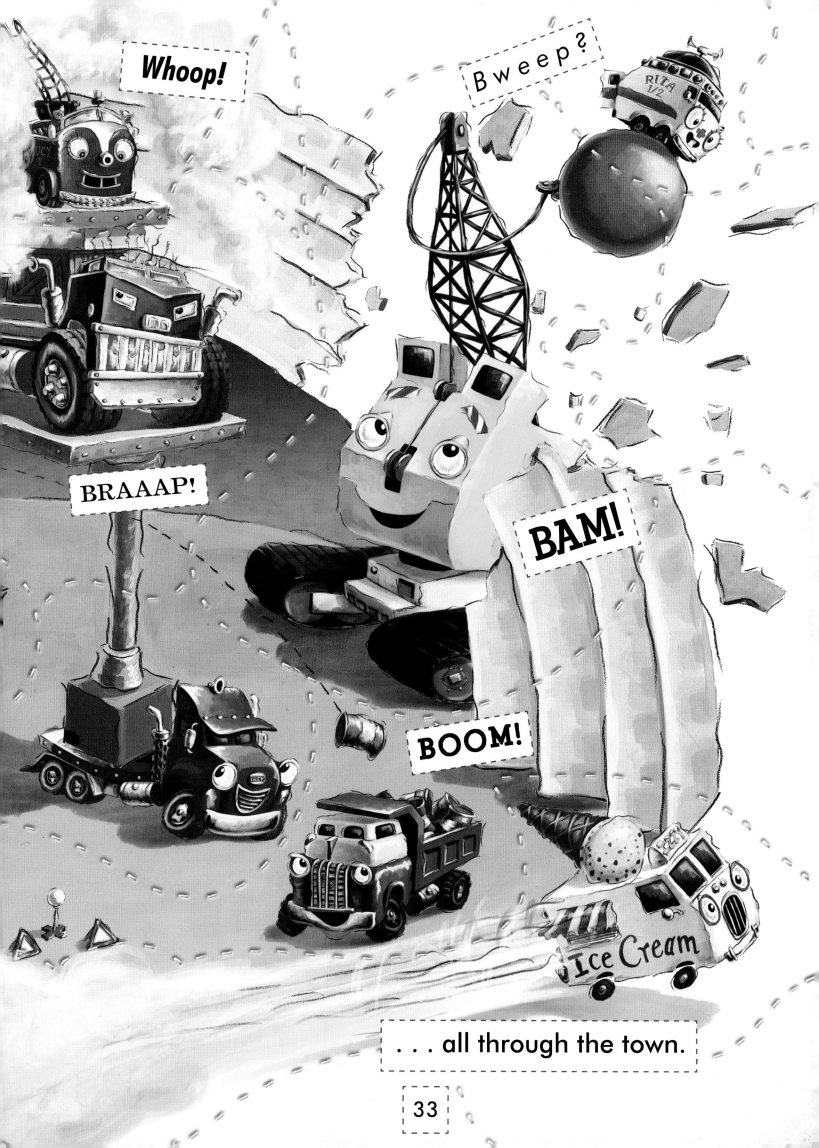

Patty cake, patty cake, Dumper Dan.

Dump me some dirt as fast as you can.

Slide it and drop it and mark it DD,

And pile it in the lot for Melvin and me.

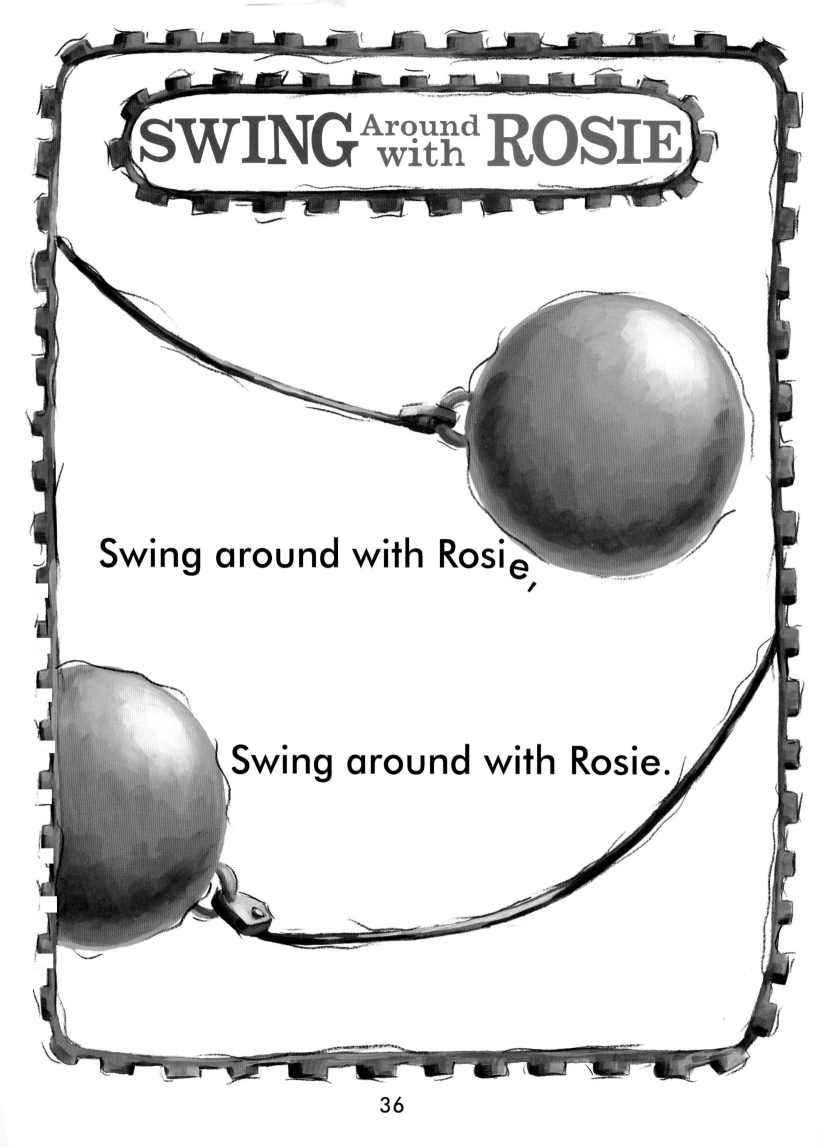

# SWING Around with ROSIE

Swing around with Rosie,

Swing around with Rosie.

# It's Raining, It's Pouring

It's raining,
it's pouring.
Monster Max is roaring.

He jumped and slid
And blew his lid
And spun around all morning.

# JACK AND KAT

Jack and Kat raced up the hill
To burn some crazy rubber.

Jack zoomed down,
Right through Trucktown,
And Kat came scraping after.

Wrecker Rosie

# Wrecker Rosie Sat on a Wall

Wrecker Rosie sat on a wall.

Wrecker Rosie made it all fall.

All the town's tow trucks

And all the town's rigs . . .

Did whatever Rosie said after that.

# This Little Truck

This little truck worried about the market.

This little truck worried about home.

This little truck worried about stop signs.

This little truck worried about mud, sharp stones,
   those icky bugs that get squashed in your grill,
   and pretty much everything else in the world.

And this worried truck honked, "Eek! Eek! Eek!"
   all the way home.

# POP! BLOWS THE DIESEL

All around the parking garage,

Pat Pumper chased the Diesel.

Pat Pumper thought it was all in truck fun,

Till **POP!** blows the Diesel.

Pat Pumper with a spool of hose,

And Lucy with her ladder.

That's the way the Truck Game goes.

POP! blows the Diesel.

# Rub-a-Dub-Dub

Rub-a-dub-dub,
three trucks in a tub.

And who do you
think they'd be?

The Pumper, the Ladder,
and little sis, Rita.
The Fire and Rescue trucks three.

# FIRE TRUCKS ARE RED

Fire trucks are red.

Max Truck is blue.

Gabby is pink.

(How about you?)

# Hey Diddle Diddle

Hey diddle diddle, the truck in the middle

Thought ice cream made up the moon.

The little truck laughed

To see such a sight

And sang his You-Know-What tune.

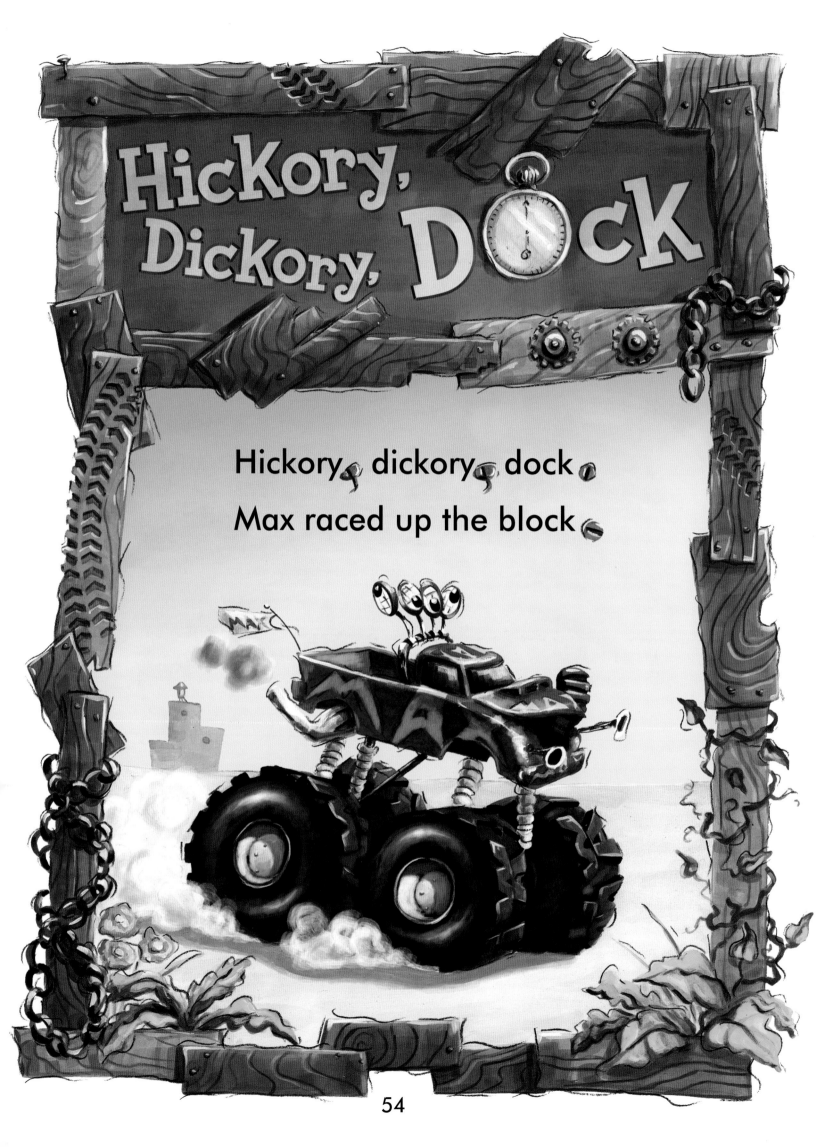

# Hickory, Dickory, Dock

Hickory, dickory, dock.
Max raced up the block.

The clock struck **one**.

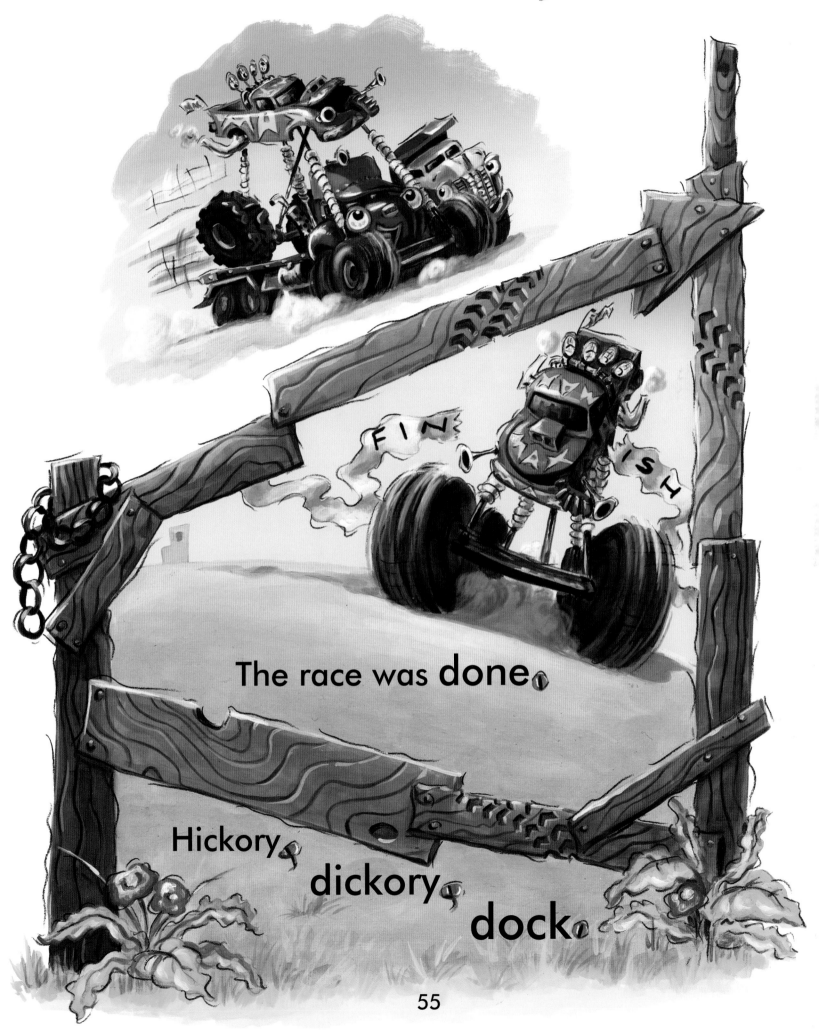

The race was **done**.

Hickory, dickory, **dock**.

# That's What **Trucks** Are Made Of

**M**etal and stuff and everything tough—
That's what trucks are made of.

Play by the **ton**, and everything **fun**—
**That's** what trucks are made of.